The Hen Who Wouldn't Give Up

JILL TOMLINSON

Pictures by Paul Howard

originally published as *Hilda the Hen*

EGMONT

For Dr Frederick N. Hicks who, like Hilda,

never gives up, and D.H. likewise

The Hen Who Wouldn't Give Up was first published in
Great Britain 1967 by Methuen and Co Ltd as *Hilda the Hen*

Published as *The Hen Who Wouldn't Give Up* 1977
by Methuen Children's Books Ltd

First published in this edition 2004 by Egmont Books Limited
This edition published 2013 by Dean,
an imprint of Egmont UK Limited
The Yellow Building, 1 Nicholas Road, London W11 4AN

ISBN 978 0 6035 6922 7

56906/1

A CIP catalogue record for this title is available from the British Library

Printed and bound in Great Britain by the CPI Group

This is Hilda.

Hilda is a small, speckled hen.

Hilda likes cornflakes,
fire-engines and
visting her auntie.

But there is one thing that
Hilda would like more than
anything else. . .

Also by Jill Tomlinson

Contents

Hilda has an
upsetting morning

Hilda was a hen – a small, brown, speckled
hen – and she lived on Biddick's Farm in a
village called Little Dollop.

Hilda was very excited. Her auntie had
just hatched out five baby chicks. Hilda was
dying to see them. The trouble was, her
auntie lived in Much Wallop, and that was

five miles away. How was Hilda going to get there? It was too far to walk.

She sat in her favourite spot under the hedge and had a good think.

Suddenly Hilda perked up her head. Of course! She would have to get a lift.

She squeezed through the hedge and hurried down the muddy lane from the farm.

There'll be lots of cars and things on the main road, she said to herself. I'll be in Much Wallop in no time. Won't Auntie be surprised to see me!

But when Hilda reached the road there was nothing in sight.

Perhaps I shall find something further on,

she thought, and set off in the direction of
Much Wallop.

She was in luck. Just around the corner
there was a row of cottages, and parked in
front of them was a big, green, lorry thing.

It was rather an odd box-like shape,
with an open half-door at the back. Hilda
hopped on to this and peered inside. She
could not see very clearly, but it seemed
to be full of torn packets and ashes and old
tins. It smelled very nasty.

Still, this was no time to be fussy. Hilda
hopped daintily down and settled on an old
cornflake packet.

There were a few cornflakes left in it.
Hilda was very fond of cornflakes.

She was just finishing the last one when
she had a terrible shock. There was a great

clanging and banging, and then a shower of horrible things was poured on top of her! She was battered and bumped by rotten apples and sticky baked-bean tins and spiky fish-bones and – ugh! – all sorts of unspeakable things. Hilda was too shocked to squawk. She thought she was going to be buried alive.

At last it stopped, but worse was to come. A voice shouted, 'All right, Bill! Up she goes!' and the whole thing began to tip up.

This helped at first, because all the rubbish rolled off Hilda again and unburied her, but it went on tipping until all the rubbish was piled at the other end of the cart, with Hilda, fluttering and furious, tumbled on top of it. It was bad enough to have dustbins emptied on her head, but to be turned upside-down as well! It was too much.

Hilda spread her wings and fluttered to the open end of the cart, which was now facing up to the sky. Just as she got there, the whole thing began to swing down again. Hilda clung desperately to the tailboard as it plunged to earth. When it stopped, she hopped down and began to run. She did not stop running until she was safely back in the farm lane again. She was shaking all over.

'Oh dear,' she clucked, collapsing into a

sad little heap by the ditch. 'Oh dear, dear!'

When she had rested a little, Hilda shook the dust out of her feathers and had a good wash in the ditch.

She felt a lot better after that.

'Silly me!' she muttered to herself as she pecked away at a patch of treacle on her tail. 'I *would* choose a rubbish cart! Never mind. I'm going to see Auntie's chicks somehow. I'll try again tomorrow – on something cleaner!'

And brave little Hilda cocked her head and set off home to the farm.

Hilda gets a lift

The sun was shining brightly when Hilda woke up next morning.

I'm sure I shall find something to take me to Much Wallop today, she thought.

She set out straight after breakfast, looking very important. Anyone could see that she was a hen who was *going* somewhere.

She went down the farm lane and along the main road towards Much Wallop. Right

through the village of Little Dollop she went, and past the few cottages on the other side, but she saw nothing she might ride on – except an old doll's pram in somebody's front garden, and that was not much good without somebody to push it.

Then she saw the very thing! It was big and red, shining in the sun – and the driver was just getting into it. There was no time to dither. One thing was certain – it was not a dust cart, and after her terrible experience of the day before, that was all that mattered to Hilda.

She would ride on this.

The extraordinary thing was that a lot of other people seemed to have the same idea! Several men jumped on to it at the same time as Hilda – men with shiny helmets. Hilda had no time to wonder why. She was too busy hanging on. The fire-engine – for that is what it was – had set off at a terrific speed. Hilda was sure she would fall off. She closed her eyes tightly as she was joggled and rattled about and the wind whistled through her feathers. The big silver bell winking in the sun above her head began to clang and clang.

It was all very exciting, and Hilda began to enjoy it. She opened her eyes and looked around her. There was a ladder just above her. She could perch more securely on that. She scrambled up to it and hopped right to the top. She had a splendid view from up there – she could see for miles.

Everything scattered in their path – carts, dogs and bicycles rushed for the shelter of the hedge when they saw, and heard, the fire-engine approaching.

Hilda was delighted. They would soon be at Much Wallop at this rate.

Then she saw to her horror that they were turning off down a side road. This was no good – she would have to get off.

'Stop!' she squawked. 'Stop! I want to get off!' But of course nobody heard her above the noise of the bell.

Then they did stop – suddenly. Hilda was nearly jerked off her perch on the top of the ladder. And the ladder began to move.

Before Hilda realised
what was happening,
she was going up and
up into the air. They
had reached the fire,
and the ladder was being
sent up to the top windows
of a very tall house so that a
fireman could climb up and rescue
anybody trapped on the top floor.
Poor Hilda wished she had a
parachute. The smoking windows were
getting nearer and nearer and she did not
want to be a cooked chicken!

Then the ladder came to rest against the
side of the house, and Hilda was relieved to
find that she was not to be tipped right into
the fire. She heard someone coming up the

ladder behind her, and was just going to look round when – whoosh! – a column of water hit the wall beside her and she was drenched.

'Oy!' shouted a voice behind. 'Watch what you're doing with the hoses down there! It's not my bath night!'

Then the fireman saw Hilda – a little huddle of wet feathers hunched at the top of the ladder.

'Hello!' he said. 'What are you doing up here, young lady? You don't look much of a fireman to me! I'll have you down in a jiffy. Just hang on while I have a look round.'

The fireman climbed over her and disappeared over the window-sill into the smoke.

He was soon back again, to Hilda's relief.

'Nobody there, my love. Come on, down we go.'

He took off his helmet and gently lifted Hilda off her perch and placed her in it. She settled down gratefully and had a comfortable ride back to earth again.

It was really awfully kind of him, particularly as she was so wet. Hilda said 'Thank you' in the only way she knew – she laid a nice brown egg in his helmet!

He felt it there when he put in his hand to lift her out.

'Well, I'm blessed!' he said, drawing it out. 'Thank you, love. That'll do fine for my tea.'

'What have you got there?' asked another fireman, coming over to look. The fire was out, and the firemen were getting back on the engine to go home. 'Good heavens! It's Hilda – from Biddick's Farm over Little Dollop way. We'd better take her home.'

So Hilda had another ride on the fire-engine – but sedately this time, in the kind fireman's helmet. He dried her as best he could with his hanky, and let the sun do the rest.

All the other firemen were jealous about the egg.

'Come on, Hilda. Lay one for us,' they teased her.

But Hilda pretended not to notice.

When they got to Little Dollop, Hilda's fireman set her down at the farm gate. She gently pecked his hand to say goodbye and then squeezed under the gate and strutted into the yard. She had created quite a sensation. It isn't every day that a hen arrives home in a fire-engine! All her friends goggled.

It was only when she had told them *all* about it that Hilda realised that her adventures were not over. She still had not

seen her auntie's new chicks at Much Wallop.

She would try again tomorrow.

Hilda has a
sticky time

Hilda's friends in the farmyard took a great interest in her at breakfast time.

'That's right, Hilda. Have a good breakfast,' said Flo, the oldest hen in the farmyard. 'You'll need to keep your pecker up!'

'You can have some of my grain if you like,' offered a little pullet shyly. 'I can't eat any more.'

'It's all right, thank you, Mary,' said

Hilda. 'I couldn't eat any more myself. Well, I must be going.' She fluffed out her feathers and started towards the gate.

'Can I come with you? Please, Hilda?' begged Mary, hopping along beside her.

'No, Mary. It's too far for you, and anyway it's difficult enough just looking after myself! I'll tell you about it when I come back. Goodbye.'

Hilda squeezed under the gate and set off down the lane.

The others crowded round the gate and watched her go.

'Good luck, Hilda,' they called. 'Give our love to your auntie!'

'I will,' Hilda called back. It was nice of them to see her off like that. She felt very happy and hopeful this morning.

Half an hour later she did not feel
anything of the kind. She had walked right
through the village and past the place where
the fire-engine had been the day before, but
still – no lift.

But as she came towards the next bend
in the road, Hilda lifted her head and sniffed.
There was a strong, hot smell in the air. She
rather liked it. When she rounded the corner,
she forgot about the smell. There was
something moving slowly along by the edge
of the road, something that she could ride on.

Hilda had never seen anything quite like
it before.

It was rather like a tractor, and it had a

huge roller at the front and a little chimney at the top with dirty smoke coming out of it. It was moving very slowly, but after her feather-raising ride on the fire-engine, this seemed to Hilda to be no bad thing. She hopped up.

The driver saw her.

'Hey! What do you want? Shoo!' he shouted.

Hilda pretended to be deaf. She stayed perched on the roof as if she had grown there.

'All right, stay there, you cheeky little bird. I'll take you home for my lunch. You'll do very nicely with a bit of stuffing.' The driver chuckled and turned back to his wheel.

Hilda felt a little alarmed at this, but she did not move. The man had a nice kindly red face; she was sure he did not really mean it.

Well, almost sure! What was important was to get to Much Wallop.

It was going to take a long time, though. Hilda had not known that anything could move as slowly as this. She could have walked faster, only her feet were so tired. Still, she would have a little rest. She closed her eyes and dozed off.

When she opened her eyes they were going the wrong way! Suddenly Hilda realised what was happening. They were going up and down over the same bit of road!

'Oh, silly me!' clucked Hilda. 'That's what the roller must be for; it's for spreading and flattening the tar to mend the road! Well, I shan't waste any more time here. I shall have to find another lift.'

She went to the back of the roof and

jumped straight down into the road.

Then the terrible thing happened. Hilda could not move! Her feet were stuck! She wriggled and tugged, but it was no good. She was stuck fast in the wet tar.

She started to peck at the tar around her feet to see if she could free them. This was a silly thing to do, as she soon realised. Her beak became stuck together with tar! The steamroller had turned round and was coming back, and she could not open her beak to warn the driver that she was there. She could not manage the tiniest squawk, and the giant roller was coming nearer and nearer. Would the driver see her?

Hilda began to flap her wings to try to attract his attention. If he did not see her – well, he would get his chicken dinner after all, and Hilda was sure he would be sorry.

He did see her. He stopped the roller and climbed down, stepping carefully along the edge of the tar.

'Well, you've got yourself into a fine pickle, haven't you?' he said, looking down at her.

Hilda hung her head in shame.

'I dunno. Some birds!' he said, shaking his head. 'Well, I'll have to get you out somehow. Wait a mo'!'

He stumped off to the roller and came back with a trowel. 'I'll have to dig you out,'

he said, 'and a fine mess that will make of my lovely flat road. You don't deserve to be rescued, my lady.'

Hilda kept very still while he eased the trowel round her feet and prised them out of the tar.

Her claws were all stuck up with it.

'Cor, you are a mess! There's only one thing to do with you.' He lifted her up gently, and carried her back to the roller. He tucked her under his arm while he poured some paraffin from a big can into his baccy tin and set it on the step.

'There now,' he said, standing Hilda in it. 'You stand in that for a while. That should do the trick. Now let's look at this beak. Hmm. You'd better dip that in, too. It won't taste very nice, but it's the best way.'

Hilda looked down at the paraffin round her ankles and shuddered. Then, brave little bird that she was, she shut her eyes, bent down, and plunged her beak into the tobacco tin.

'There's a good girl,' said the driver with admiration. 'That's enough now. Let's see.'

He took Hilda's beak in his hands and gently pulled it apart. Then he rubbed it with a paraffin rag until it was quite free from tar. Hilda clucked quietly in her throat.

The driver lifted Hilda on to his lap and dried her feet thoroughly.

'There you are, you troublesome little baggage. You'd better run along home before I change my mind about that chicken dinner. Go on! Shoo!'

He set her down and shooed her back along the road to Little Dollop. Then he took a trowelful of tar and went back to fill in the holes that Hilda's feet had made in the new road.

When he was safely out of the way, Hilda crept back. He had been very nice to her and she wanted to leave him a present. That done, she set off home.

When the driver came back, he found a nice brown egg beside his baccy tin.

'Well, there's a thing!' he said, looking down the road after her. 'Thank you, little lady.'

The little lady was teased dreadfully when she got home.

'Back already, Hilda? That was a short visit!'

'Oooh, Hilda! You smell awful! Go and have a bath in the horse trough, for goodness' sake!'

Hilda did have a bath in the horse trough, but paraffin is a very *clingy* sort of smell and the others went on being very rude.

'Never mind,' said little Mary consolingly. 'It'll soon wear off.'

'Yes,' said Hilda. 'And you know, there's one good thing about it. I am learning what *not* to get a lift on, and that's very useful.'

Hilda goes
out to tea

All the farmyard came to see Hilda off again
next day. They teased her a bit, but she did
not mind. She squeezed under the gate and
turned to say goodbye.

'You be careful now, my girl,' said old
Flo. 'Watch where you're putting your feet.'

'And do try not to choose anything
smelly,' pleaded Clarissa.

'You wait – I shall smell *lovely* this time,'

said Hilda. 'Goodbye now.'

'Goodbye, Hilda. Good luck!' they called after her.

Hilda *was* luckier this morning. At least she thought she was. There was something parked outside the very first row of cottages. It was a little red and white motor scooter. It was very small, but it had a double saddle, and there would be room for Hilda on that. Under the saddle was a big card with 'L' written on it, but Hilda did not know what that meant.

The proud owner came out of one of the cottages at that moment. It was Miss Smith, the teacher from Little Dollop school. She was wearing an enormous crash helmet. She sat gingerly on the saddle and began to kick at the starter.

Hilda, who had hidden by the hedge until Miss Smith was safely mounted, now crept forward and hopped up on to the saddle. Miss Smith was much too busy to notice her. This was the very first time she had taken the scooter on the road. She had practised a bit in the garden and that was about all.

She kicked the starter a little harder and suddenly the engine burst into life. The scooter made two leaps forward like a learner kangaroo, and then shot off in a cloud of smoke with Miss Smith – and Hilda – hanging on for dear life. In fact, it would be hard to say who was the more frightened – Hilda or Miss Smith herself!

Miss Smith was finding it very difficult to steer. They zigzagged along, one minute careering down the middle of the road, the

next heading straight for the ditch. Hilda
closed her eyes – she could not bear to look.

They also wobbled. Poor Miss Smith.
The more she wobbled,
the more she zigzagged,
and the more she
zigzagged, the
more she
wobbled.

For Hilda it was
like being in a small
boat on a rough sea.
She began to feel sea-sick.

Round the next bend was a bumpy bit of road. They began to bounce. It was too much for Hilda. At the second bounce she opened her beak and let out a loud squawk!

That was too much for Miss Smith. What was crouching behind her? She wobbled violently, lost control, and drove straight through the hedge.

Luckily they were passing Journey's End Farm at the time, and their journey ended in the middle of a haystack!

When Hilda picked herself up, she felt a bit giddy and stupid and she still had her eyes tight shut. When she realised that at last she was on firm ground again – no more joggling and bouncing – she felt brave enough to open her eyes.

There was a strange mushroom thing

wriggling on the ground by the fallen scooter.

It was poor Miss Smith! Her helmet was jammed right down to her chin and she was wrestling with it to get it off.

Hilda thought that this might be a good moment to disappear. She had tiptoed away only a few yards when, with a sound like a popping cork, Miss Smith emerged from her helmet. She saw Hilda.

'A hen!' she gasped. 'Only a hen! Oh, you did frighten me! Come here! You ought to be ashamed of yourself. What were you doing on my scooter?'

Hilda hung her head. Her feathers were still all ruffled, and bits of hay and chaff were stuck all over her.

Miss Smith looked down at herself. She was just as bad.

'Well, don't just stand there,' she said. 'We must help each other to tidy up.'

So Hilda, who had decided that Miss Smith's bark was worse than her bite, came over and started to peck the bits of straw from Miss Smith's jumper, while Miss Smith picked Hilda's feathers clean. As they worked, Miss Smith gave Hilda a lecture.

'Now, Miss Hen – I hope you've learned your lesson. Never take a ride on something without *asking* first. If I had known you were there, this accident would never have happened. If you want somebody to give you a lift, you must stand by the road and hold your claw up, like this.'

Miss Smith held up her fist and pointed her thumb down the road. 'You see? It's called hitch-hiking, and all drivers understand

it. You point your thumb – all right, claw –
in the direction in which you want to go,
and then if the driver has the time, he will
stop and pick you up. You understand?'

Hilda nodded. If only she had known
before! Tomorrow she would try it.

'Well,' said Miss Smith, standing up and
brushing down her skirt, 'I think we'll do now.
My scooter seems to be all right. I'll give you
a lift home if you like.'

Hilda didn't like! She was not going
through all that again. She backed away.

'It's all right,' said Miss Smith, laughing.
'I think I've had enough for one day, too. I
shall *push* it home.'

That was different. Hilda waited while
Miss Smith righted the scooter and then she
hopped up on the back again. They had a

pleasant journey home. Hilda liked Miss Smith.

When they reached her cottage, Miss Smith propped her scooter against the fence.

'Here we are,' she said. 'Oh, I'm dying for a cup of tea.'

Hilda hopped down and looked hopefully at Miss Smith.

Miss Smith was a very understanding person. 'You must be thirsty, too, Miss Hen. Would you care to join me for a cup of tea?'

Hilda had never been invited out to tea before. She followed Miss Smith into her kitchen. Miss Smith put the kettle on and then looked down at Hilda.

'I don't expect tea is much good to you, is it? Let me see what I can find.'

Hilda liked what she found. Miss Smith brought her a cup of water, some porridge oats, and – how could Miss Smith have known? – some cornflakes.

Hilda decided she liked going out to tea.

'Well, you're a very tidy eater, I must say,' said Miss Smith, looking at her clean kitchen floor when Hilda had finished. She hadn't left a crumb. 'You must come again one day.'

Miss Smith saw Hilda to the door. 'I hope you know your way home from here, Miss Hen. Well, goodbye. Remember what I told you – *ask* next time. Goodbye.'

Hilda went down the path and out of the front gate. She paused for a few minutes to leave something for Miss Smith in her upturned crash helmet, and then made for Little Dollop and the farm.

When she reached the gate, everyone rushed to welcome her.

'Hilda! Did you get to Much Wallop?'

'No, I'm afraid not. But I've been to tea with Miss Smith the school teacher.'

'You *haven't*!' They couldn't believe it. Hilda told them all about it.

Then old Flo came up and sniffed her.

'Well, I never! She smells lovely! Come and smell her, girls.' They gathered round and sniffed cautiously.

Hilda smelled faintly of Miss Smith's lavender water.

'I told you I would come home smelling nice,' she said.

Hilda goes
hitch-hiking

The following morning, Hilda preened her feathers with special care. She was going to hitch-hike properly today, and she was sure no driver would stop for a *scruffy* hen.

She was just putting the finishing touches to her tail, when Clarissa burst into the henhouse, flapping her wings with a lot of fuss and shaking her untidy head. She looked across at Hilda.

'Well, you're wasting your time,' she said. 'It's raining.'

Hilda quietly went on working at her tail.

'Did you hear what I said?' demanded Clarissa. 'It's pouring with rain. Half the yard is flooded. You'll have mud up to your wish-bone by the time you reach the gate!'

Hilda shuddered. Clarissa did use such vulgar expressions!

'I can at least start out looking respectable,' she said, 'and my feathers will be far more waterproof if they're properly arranged.'

'You're just a fusspot,' said Clarissa.

Hilda cocked a bright eye at her. She was tempted to say something about moth-eaten old boilers, but she sensibly kept it back.

When Hilda was ready, she stepped out of the henhouse door. Clarissa was right about the rain; it was a very wet day indeed. Hilda picked her way carefully across the yard, trying to avoid the puddles.

There was nobody to see her off today except a few ducks, and they were much too busy enjoying themselves to take much notice of her. One gentleman duck did bow to her as she went past, and said, 'Lovely day, what?' but that was all.

When she reached the road, Hilda stationed herself under a large tree which gave her some shelter from the rain, and practised thumbing a lift. It was really quite difficult to balance on one claw and gesture with the other. She fell over several times before she got it right.

She tried it on a green sports car at first, but the driver did not even see her.

I wish I were white, she thought. Speckly brown isn't a very showing-up sort of colour.

After two more cars had gone straight past without stopping or even slowing down, Hilda began to feel a bit hopeless. Who was going to bother to stop and pick up a small soggy hen in this weather?

But somebody did. Just when Hilda was almost ready to give up, she saw a lorry coming. She decided to have one last try. The lorry was not going very fast, and as it came nearer, Hilda got ready. As it drew abreast of her, she fluttered up on to the bonnet and perched there on one claw, hopefully waggling the other one in the direction of Much Wallop.

The driver peered unbelievingly through the windscreen-wipers. A hitch-hiking hen! He had occasionally given lifts to husky young men with shorts and rucksacks – but a *hen*!

He stopped the lorry, slammed down the window and poked his head out into the rain.

'Well, hello there! D'you want a lift to Much Wallop? Come on then – you'd better come in before you're washed away.'

Hilda was so relieved. She hopped on to the enormous hand the young man had thrust out for her, and allowed herself to be drawn inside the cab.

'My, you are wet!' he said kindly, setting Hilda down beside him on the seat. 'I'll put the heater on for a bit.'

He closed the window and turned a knob on the dashboard. They started off and soon there was a comforting wave of warm air filling the cab. After a few minutes Hilda was steaming like a little engine.

'Well, this is very nice,' the young man said. 'I like a bit of company when I'm driving. It stops me going to sleep.'

They drove on for a little while.

Hilda began to get a bit worried. They must be nearing Much Wallop now. Her auntie's farm was just this side of the village, and she did not know how to tell the young man where she wanted to get off.

She hopped on to his lap and jiggled up and down, peering out of the window and clucking gently.

'What's this, then?' said the young man. 'You want to tell me where I'm to put you down, is that it? Well, you squawk good and loud when we get there, and I'll stop for you. All right?'

Hilda nodded. She watched for the two white posts outside Auntie's farm.

There they were! Hilda squawked.

The young man pulled up so sharply that he nearly shot Hilda through the windscreen.

'There you are. How about that for service? It's stopped raining for you, too.

Mind how you go, now.'

The young man opened the door and helped Hilda down the step.

'Wait a minute, though – how are you going to get home?'

Hilda cocked her head on one side and looked hopefully up at him.

'You want me to take you home, do you?' chuckled the young man. 'I dunno – these modern hens! Well, as it happens, I shall be passing about tea-time. If you're waiting for me here, by the posts, at five o'clock, I'll pick you up. All right? Bye-bye, then. Be seeing you.' He slammed the door and the lorry rumbled off.

Hilda looked across at the farm and sighed with happiness. She was here at last!

She looked carefully both ways and

crossed the road. There was a little group of hens just by the gate.

'Er – excuse me,' Hilda said. 'I'm looking for my aunt – a Mrs Emma Hen.'

'Oh, you'll find her in the field over there with her new family,' said one of the hens. 'Just through that white fence.' She pointed to a field with a lot of white coops dotted about.

Hilda thanked her and hurried excitedly across. She squeezed under the fence and looked about her. Which of the coops was Auntie's? There were so many of them, all exactly alike.

Just at that moment, the farmer's little girl began to go down the rows of coops, letting out the hens for their morning exercise. In a few minutes the field was full of proud mothers with their families in tow, like fat kites with long yellow tails jerking in the wind. Each family of little chicks lined up one behind the other after their mother, and wherever she went, no matter how many times she changed direction, they followed in scuttling procession.

Hilda was just wondering how she would find Auntie among all these hens, when one kite broke away from the rest and came rushing to meet her.

'Hilda! How lovely to see you!'

It was Aunt Emma, and behind her tumbled one, two, three, four, five little pom-poms, all cheeping hard.

Well, Hilda *was* glad that she had come. There were no chicks on Biddick's Farm; Mary was the youngest, and she was a pullet – a sort of teenager hen. Hilda had never seen chicks at close hand before, and she loved them. Chicks were fun.

They thought Hilda was fun, too! She played all sorts of games with them. Their favourite was a chasing game. Their mother had to run about with the chicks streaming behind her, twisting and dodging, while the 'fox' – Hilda – tried to catch the littlest one at the end of the line. The chicks 'cheeeeeeeeped!' with excitement as Hilda chased them and pounced again and again. She always missed – until the littlest one began to get caught on purpose.

Then Auntie, who hadn't any breath left, suggested a nice *quiet* game. So they played

Follow My Leader while their mother had a nice rest.

And when they were tired out, the chicks demanded a story. So Hilda settled them around her and told them all about her week's adventures. She told them about the dust cart, and the fire-engine, and the steamroller, and Miss Smith's scooter and the lorry . . .

'Goodness!' she said when she got to that bit. 'That young man said he would pick me up at about five! I must fly.'

'Oh, not yet! Tell us another story, Hilda, *please* tell us another story,' begged the chicks.

'You're a great success,' said Auntie, as they all saw Hilda to the fence. 'It's the first peaceful afternoon I've had since they hatched. Please come and see us again.'

'Yes, please do, please do,' chanted the chicks, bobbing up and down.

'Well, I'll do my best,' Hilda said, 'but you know how it is. I did have a *little* difficulty getting here this time!'

Hilda goes broody

Hilda *had* loved those chicks. For days after
visiting them she could think and talk about
nothing else.

'They were so sweet,' she told the
henhouse for what must have been the
hundredth time, 'so soft and fluffy and
cuddly. Oh, they were *adorable*.'

Everybody went on scratching – which
is rather rude when someone is speaking.

The other hens were just a little tired of Auntie's chicks.

Hilda sighed and wandered out into the yard. She scratched half-heartedly at a bit of chaff, but she was not really interested. Chicks – little yellow chicks – that was all she could think about.

She fluffed out her feathers and tried to imagine what it would feel like to have lots of downy babies jostling under her wings.

Oh, it would be nice to have a family of her very own.

She wandered down the lane at the back of the farm. She had not been there for quite some time, and was surprised to see two little white lambs bouncing all over the meadow at the bottom.

Their mother, Sophie, came over to the

fence to speak to her.

'Good morning, Hilda,' she said. 'You haven't met my family yet, have you? This is Plain and this is Purl.'

'Baa-aa-aa!' said Plain and Purl together, stopping their dance for an instant. Then they were off again, catkin tails a-waggle.

'They're charming,' said Hilda wistfully. She gave a big sigh.

'Why Hilda, whatever's the matter?' asked Sophie kindly. 'You don't seem a bit yourself this morning.'

'I'm not,' Hilda said miserably. 'I feel most peculiar. I've gone off my food and I feel all droopy – and all I can think about is chicks.'

'Is that all!' laughed Sophie. 'Well, that's easily cured. You're just broody, that's all.'

'Broody?' Hilda said.

'Yes. It's very common in hens. What you need is – excuse me . . .'

Sophie turned on the twins who were bouncing round her in the most irritating way. 'For goodness' sake! Either stay up or stay down!'

She turned back to Hilda. 'I'm so sorry. They make me quite dizzy. What was I saying? Oh yes. What you need is a family of your own.'

'Well, I know *that*,' Hilda said peevishly.

'Then instead of brooding about it, why don't you?'

'Why don't I what?'

'Have a family, you silly goose – I mean hen!'

Hilda lifted her head and looked at Sophie.

'Oh, silly, silly me!' she said. 'Of course! That's what I'll do. Thank you, Sophie.'

So next morning Hilda began her family.

It was a small beginning: just a little brown egg at the bottom of her nesting-box. She laid one like it every day.

But today, instead of going off to the

yard with the others to have breakfast, she stayed behind in the henhouse to look after the egg. She settled herself down on it, spreading her soft under-feathers over it carefully. She must keep it warm if it was to hatch out into her first chick.

She sat with her eyes closed, planning how she could lay one every day until she had five or six to hatch.

Mrs Biddick, the farmer's wife, found her there when she came to collect the eggs.

'Hilda? Don't you want any breakfast, you silly bird?' Mrs Biddick thought all hens were silly – even Hilda!

Hilda sat tight.

'Hilda! Come on. Get up, you lazy old thing. I want your egg.'

Hilda knew she did; that's why she wasn't

moving! Mrs Biddick was not going to have *this* egg.

'Oh, Hilda, you haven't gone broody on me. If there's one thing I cannot abide, it's a broody hen. Come on now – hand over!'

Hilda fluffed out her feathers and looked as fierce as she could.

Now it wasn't the first time Mrs Biddick had had to deal with a broody hen. She turned her back on Hilda as if she had given up and busied herself collecting the eggs from the other nesting-boxes.

Hilda relaxed again and continued with her dream. Yes – five or six would make a nice little family.

But before Hilda realised what was happening, Mrs Biddick had turned again, thrust a swift, practised hand under her and taken the precious egg. There it was, lying on top of all those *ordinary* eggs in Mrs Biddick's basket.

'I'm very sorry, Hilda,' said Mrs Biddick as she went towards the door. 'You're one of my best layers. I just can't afford to let you sit.'

Hilda wasn't listening. Her eyes were on that egg on top of the basket. She was not going to let it out of her sight.

She hopped down from her box and followed Mrs Biddick at a safe distance.

Follow that egg!

Mrs Biddick took the basket of eggs straight across the yard and handed it to Mr Biddick, who was loading the milk truck outside the dairy. The Biddicks had a small milk round and supplied milk and eggs to most of Little Dollop.

'Thank you, m'dear,' said Mr Biddick, taking the basket and wedging it carefully between two big churns at the back of the truck. 'How many today?'

'Only twenty-three,' Mrs Biddick said, 'and now it looks as though Hilda's going broody.'

'Aye – she's been a bit restless lately.'

Hilda was more than a bit restless – she was frantic! The egg must be getting *so* cold, exposed to the air like that. She hopped up and down anxiously behind the truck, and as soon as Mrs Biddick had gone back to the house and her husband had his back turned, Hilda jumped up into the truck and crouched behind a big churn. Mr Biddick brought out the last churn, fastened the tailboard and went round to the driving cab.

Before he even had the engine running, Hilda was on that basket. It wasn't very comfortable; twenty-three eggs are a lot of eggs for one small hen. In the end she concentrated upon keeping *her* egg warm –

and on keeping her balance! The truck
bounced her up and down like a tennis-ball.

Mr Biddick pulled up outside the first row
of cottages in Little Dollop, and came round
to the back to get ready to serve. Hilda
slithered off her lumpy couch and retreated
behind her churn.

Mr Biddick's customers came out to the
truck carrying jugs for their milk and basins
for their eggs.

'Nice morning, Mr Biddick!' said the first customer. 'I'll have my usual half-pint, please.'

Hilda knew that voice. She peeped out. Yes, it was her friend Miss Smith! She watched as Mr Biddick plunged his long-handled measuring dipper into the churn and poured half a pint of fresh, new milk into Miss Smith's jug.

'Oh, and two eggs, please,' added Miss Smith.

Mr Biddick's large hand descended upon the basket of eggs. Hilda shut her eyes. She knew what was going to happen.

She was right. When she opened her eyes again, her egg was gone. Mr Biddick had put it into Miss Smith's basin!

It was a nice basin, with blue and white stripes, but that was no comfort to Hilda seeing that her family was being carried off in it.

Still, at least she knew where it was going. She could follow it to Miss Smith's as soon as she could get away from the truck without being seen.

At last everybody had been served. Mr Biddick put up the tailboard and prepared to drive off. Hilda slipped down from the truck and scuttled into the hedge. As the back of the truck disappeared down the road, Hilda flew up Miss Smith's path.

The back door was shut. So was the kitchen window, but it had a fairly wide sill. Hilda stood back, took a little run, and jumped up to it. Then she tapped urgently on the window with her beak.

Miss Smith jumped. She had been baking, and she was scraping the mixing bowl with a wooden spoon and having a very undignified lick. She was quite relieved to see that it was only Hilda at the window.

'Why – it's Miss Hen. Do come in.' Miss Smith threw open the window.

It opened outwards, and Hilda was knocked flying! Miss Smith hurriedly opened the door – and promptly sat on the mat with a bump as Hilda dived between her legs and knocked them from under her.

'Help!' cried Miss Smith. 'What on earth is the matter?'

Hilda was rushing wildly round the kitchen with rolling eyes. *Where was that basin?*

Ah – there it was, on the table. She jumped up, knocking over the flour bin as she did so, and scrambled awkwardly on to the basin. At last! She was with her family again. She settled herself as comfortably as she could.

Miss Smith shook the flour out of her eyes and looked at Hilda, plomped on the basin like a lopsided tea-cosy.

'Have you finished?' she asked acidly. 'Is it safe to get up now?'

Hilda just blinked happily.

Miss Smith picked herself up and cleared away the mess. Then she put on the kettle for a cup of tea. She felt she needed it.

She looked across at Hilda.

'Miss Hen – would you mind telling me

what's so special about that basin? It's empty, you know.'

Hilda looked up at her in horror. She backed awkwardly off the basin and looked into it. There was nothing there at all.

Well, where was the egg then? She began to run round the table, searching for it.

Suddenly Miss Smith understood.

'Oh, Miss Hen! Was one of those eggs yours? Was it very special?'

Hilda took her head out of the sugar packet and looked at Miss Smith.

'Oh dear! What have I done?' Miss Smith felt like a murderer. 'I'm afraid it's in – there.' She pointed to the oven door. A delicious smell had been filling the kitchen for some time.

'I've put your egg into a – into a Victoria sponge!'

Hilda couldn't believe it. She sank on to the table like last year's hat.

Miss Smith looked round wildly for some way of comforting her.

'Oh dear. Er – have some cornflakes!' She grabbed a packet of cornflakes from the dresser and poured a small mountain of them at Hilda's feet.

Hilda looked pained. Cornflakes! At a time like this.

Still – she had not had any breakfast. Perhaps just one or two . . .

As the mountain went down, Hilda's spirits went up. All was not lost. She could lay another egg tomorrow. And this time she would make sure that Mrs Biddick didn't find it!

By the time the mountain had disappeared, Hilda was her perky self again.

Nevertheless, Miss Smith thought it best to see Hilda out of the front door before taking the sponge out of the oven.

It was a beautiful sponge, but poor Miss Smith could not bring herself to eat it. She would have felt like a cannibal.

She gave it to the vicar for the Brownie fête.

The burglar

Hilda had a terrible time trying to find a secret place in which to have her family. Again and again she was discovered and her eggs were taken away.

Mind you, Hilda chose some very silly places: the dog-kennel for instance. She might have known that Old Bailey wouldn't put up with that for long. It was not a very big kennel and Bailey was a very big dog.

He didn't *want* a lodger.

Hilda was pushed out, egg and all. Mrs Biddick spotted it from the kitchen door – and that was the end of that one.

Then there was the old cap of Mr Biddick's that Hilda found on a shelf in a dark corner of the barn. It was very warm and comfortable, and Mr Biddick did not wear it often, but he *did* wear it when it rained.

And one morning when Hilda had to leave her family for a few minutes to pop out for a snack – she had to eat sometimes – it began to rain. Mr Biddick, his mind on pigs and sheep and such (he was going to market) came in hurriedly and slapped the cap on his head.

It only had two eggs in it, but he was not very pleased. Egg shampoos are all very well, but not at nine o'clock in the morning on market day!

The pig trough was not a very bright choice, either. You can't expect pigs to stop eating for three weeks just to oblige a broody hen. In any case, Mr Biddick came along every morning and poured a couple of buckets of pig swill into it.

Horrible stuff, pig swill, with all sorts of nasty things floating in it. Mr Biddick got his own back there all right!

Hilda retired to the hedge to clean up, and then had a good think. Where else could she try? She had tried every possible – and impossible – place in and around the farm buildings.

Of course, there was always the farm-house itself. Hilda had never been inside . . .

That evening Mrs Biddick went to bed before her husband. He was going to have a nice long soak in the bath and do his accounts. He could always do sums best in the bath.

'You go on, m'dear,' he said. 'I'll try not to wake you when I come in.'

Mrs Biddick was tired. She climbed into bed after her hot water bottle and snuggled down. She was almost asleep when she heard the noise.

It was a sort of stirring sound, and it came from under the bed!

Mrs Biddick lay there in the dark, her eyes wide open, listening. There it was again. No doubt about it, there was somebody there.

Mrs Biddick was braver than most of us. She took a deep breath, leaned out and peeped under the bed.

There was an eye looking at her.

Mrs Biddick didn't feel brave any more.

'Help!' she screamed. 'Ben! Ben!'

She made an enormous leap from the bed to the door, fearful that 'it' would grab her leg as she went past, and bumped into something huge and wet and slippery.

'Help!' screamed Mrs Biddick at the top of her voice.

'I *am* helping,' said Mr Biddick. 'Or at least I would be, m'dear, if you would just take your head out of my stomach.'

'Oh Ben! It's you.' Mrs Biddick detached herself from her dripping husband. 'Ben – there's a burglar under the bed.'

'Is that all! You got me out of a perfectly good bath just for a burglar?'

'No, Ben, really. I saw his eyes. I know there's somebody there.'

Mr Biddick sighed, girded up his towel and strode over to the bed.

'Burglar!' he said firmly. 'Come out. I'm sorry, but my wife insists.'

Nothing happened.

Mr Biddick bent down and poked his head underneath the bed.

The burglar looked at Mr Biddick, and Mr Biddick looked at the burglar.

Mr Biddick retreated. 'I'm not putting my hand in there!' he said.

'Why not?' asked Mrs Biddick, wide-eyed. 'What's under there?'

'Well, you never know with burglars. She might peck me.'

'Hilda!' said Mrs Biddick. 'It's that hen, isn't it? That does it. She's going in the pot. In the pot, first thing in the morning. You wait, my girl!' Mrs Biddick looked about for a weapon.

Hilda decided not to wait. She scuttled between Mr Biddick's wet feet, dodged Mrs Biddick's hair-brush, and scooted down the landing. She practically flew down the banisters and into the kitchen. She hid under the table.

Mr Biddick took the hair-brush from Mrs Biddick's trembling hand and made soothing noises.

'There now, my luvver. Easy now. I'll get my dressing-gown on and make you a nice cup of tea.'

He went downstairs and put the kettle on. Very quietly, he opened the back door and let the burglar out.

'Hop it,' he whispered, 'or there'll be chicken soup for dinner tomorrow!'

Hilda hopped.

Mr Biddick was just about to pour out the tea when there was a terrible shriek from upstairs, followed immediately by strange thumps.

Mr Biddick put down the teapot and went upstairs to investigate.

'Not *another* burglar!' he said, putting his head round the door.

It was not another burglar. It was just

that Mrs Biddick had decided to join her husband in the kitchen, and had started to put on her dressing-gown and slippers.

And Hilda had left one of her family in the left slipper, and Mrs Biddick had not noticed it until it was too late.

She was hopping about trying to find somewhere to put her sticky foot. The eggshell was sharp and she couldn't put her foot down, but she couldn't step out of the slipper because of the mess it would make on the carpet.

Mr Biddick was a great help.

'Trust you to put your foot in it, maid,' he said, grinning all over his face.

At that moment Mrs Biddick knew exactly what to do with her eggy slipper.

She was a good shot. Mr Biddick had to get back in the bath.

Hilda is
really brave

Next morning Hilda ran away.

She did not really run away – not for good, that is. She intended to come back again when she had hatched out her family.

It was just that she thought it might be a good idea to get out of Mrs Biddick's way for a while! She thought that she might have more chance of keeping her eggs if she laid them away from the farm altogether.

By milking time Hilda was far across the fields, out of sight of the farm. This time she must find a really good place for her nest. She squeezed under gates and hedges, and inspected every ditch.

Hilda knew exactly what she wanted.

It had to be somewhere that was safe from people – like farmers with buckets.

It had to be a place that did not belong to somebody else who might want it back – no more kennels or caps or slippers.

Above all, it had to be where Mrs Biddick could not find it. Even if she did not put Hilda in the pot, she would take away the eggs to sell – and Hilda was determined that *this* family should not end up in a Victoria sponge!

Hilda knew exactly what she needed – and she found it at the end of an old overgrown cart track which looked as if nobody had been down it for years. Grass was growing down the middle, and brambles and nettles pressed in from either side.

And at the end of it, beyond a broken gate, was an old cottage.

There was no door to the cottage. Like the windows, it was just a gaping hole. Much of the roof had fallen in, and the crumbling walls looked as if *they* would fall down if the tall, strong weeds which were holding them up were to let go for a minute. Nobody had lived in it for a very long time and it was unlikely that anybody would ever want to do so again – except, perhaps, a little speckled hen.

Hilda threaded her way through the weeds excitedly and peeped inside.

The cottage was just an empty shell, but

the corner on the left of the doorway was curtained with cobwebs, and propped against the wall was an old mattress. Hilda picked her way across the dusty, rotten floor and looked behind it.

There, black with age but with the handle still firmly attached, was an old frying-pan.

What better place to make her nest? Hilda tried it for size, patting round and round and then settling in it.

It fitted; it might have been made for her. Hilda had found her secret place. Nobody would think of looking for her here.

Hilda shifted uncomfortably in the hard frying-pan. It could do with a bit of padding. Then she looked up at the mattress. Well, that was not going to be very difficult to arrange. She tugged at some loose stuffing with her sharp beak, and soon her new home had a nice warm lining.

Now she was ready to have her family.

By the end of the week, Hilda had laid six eggs. Then she decided to stop. There wasn't really room for more in the frying-pan and she could get them all tucked neatly under her. If she had another, there would always be one left out in the cold.

Now all she had to do was sit – and sit – and sit. It was very boring. And lonely. She longed for a good gossip with someone. She was getting hungry, too. There was really very little for a hen to eat around the cottage, except for a worm or two.

She was sitting there one morning, dreaming of cornflakes – mountains and mountains of cornflakes – when she thought she heard a car.

It was a car. And three lorries, and a bulldozer and an enormous earth-excavator on caterpillar treads. It sounded like a tank as it rumbled past the cottage. It shook the old walls to their foundations even before they began to knock them down.

For that is what they had come to do, the men in the lorries. They were going to knock down Hilda's cottage and level the land around it to make room for twenty new houses.

Of course, all that poor Hilda knew was that once again her family was in danger. She sat frozen behind her mattress screen as boots scrunched on the path, came inside, walked round and went out again. What on earth was going on?

She soon found out. There were bumps

and thumps on the roof. Then came a shattering crash as a hatchet bit into a beam. Then another and another.

They were tearing down the roof.

Hilda was terrified. She wanted to run away, but she could not do that. She couldn't leave her family. She was going to keep *this* family if it killed her.

It nearly did. Soon there were beams crashing down. And slates. And bricks. Only Hilda's mattress saved her. Beams fell across it, slates bounced off it, plaster coated it; it was soon almost buried in dust. But Hilda remained unharmed beneath it – dusty, and very frightened, but unharmed.

Then they began to knock down the walls. The noise was deafening. Hilda felt battered and bludgeoned by it. The floor beneath her shook with every crash. It was like being in an earthquake.

Hilda wanted to run. She wanted to terribly, but she didn't. Being brave isn't not being frightened. It is being frightened and still not running away.

And Hilda was really brave. She sat there guarding her eggs while the walls fell down – and she didn't run.

Then Harry found her.

Harry was supposed to be knocking down Hilda's wall – it was the only one left standing – but he had stopped for a breather. He bent down to tuck a flapping trouser leg in his boot, and saw Hilda's eye gleaming from under the mattress.

Harry thought it must be a cat at first.
He moved a beam to take a closer look – and
there was Hilda.

Harry could not believe his eyes. He
called his foreman.

'Here, George! Come and see what I've
found!'

George scrambled over the rubble and peered behind the mattress.

'Crikey!' he said. 'A hen. D'you mean to say she's been sitting here through all this?' He waved his arm at the wreckage.

'She must have been, poor little blighter. Deserves a medal, that's what she does. She must be sitting – wouldn't leave her eggs.'

'Well, she can't stay here. They'll be coming to clear this lot in a minute.'

Harry looked down at brave little Hilda.

'Look, George – couldn't we leave her – just until her eggs hatch out? I mean, after all she's been through . . .'

'Oh, come off it, Harry. We can't hold up a whole housing scheme just for a hen. Families have been waiting for these houses for months.'

'Well, what about *her* family? She's done her best for it, hasn't she?'

Hilda liked Harry.

But George had his job to do – and he had noticed something.

'Look, Harry, we don't have to turn her off her nest. Look what she's sitting in! We can move her, family and all. Here, hang on to this mattress!'

George crawled under the mattress and backed out very carefully with the frying-pan and its contents.

Hilda was still very dazed, but she tried to look as dignified as possible.

A voice came from the other side of the wall.

'Isn't anybody doing any work around here? Where's George?'

George hurriedly handed the frying-pan to Harry.

'Here – take it. She's all yours.'

'What shall I do with her?'

'I don't know. You're the one who wanted to give her a medal.' George hurried off.

Harry and Hilda looked at each other.

'I suppose I'll just have to take you home,' said Harry.

Hilda's family

Harry felt pretty silly carrying the frying-pan across the building site – and did his friends laugh!

But this was nothing to what Harry's landlady had to say when he got Hilda home.

'You're not bringing that fowl in here! Just think what she'll do to my clean carpets!'

'But she's sitting,' poor Harry pleaded. 'She's going to have a family.'

'Not in here, she isn't. You know the rules
– No Pets Allowed!'

'I could put newspaper down,' Harry
said, 'and she could stay in my room . . .'

'No!' said the landlady.

So Harry and the frying-pan and Hilda
went down the main street of Little Dollop in
search of a home.

And whom should they meet but Miss
Smith! She was just coming out of the village
shop and she *was* surprised to see Hilda
approaching in a frying-pan!

'Hello, Miss Hen! Hitch-hiking again?'

Harry beamed at Miss Smith. 'You know
her, Miss? You know who she belongs to?'

'Yes. She comes from Biddick's Farm.
Hilda and I are old friends, aren't we, Hilda?'

Hilda clucked in her throat. Miss Smith

looked at Harry.

'The Biddicks have been looking for her everywhere. Where did you find her?'

Harry explained about the building site. 'Deserves a medal, she does,' he finished.

'I think she would most probably prefer some cornflakes,' said Miss Smith. Hilda brightened considerably. 'I had better take her home with me. I shall be seeing Mr Biddick in the morning when he comes with the milk.'

Harry – with relief – handed Hilda over to Miss Smith.

'I hope Mr Biddick will let her keep the eggs,' he said. 'She deserves to, after sticking by them like that.'

'I hope so, too,' said Miss Smith. 'I shall do my best to persuade him.'

So Hilda went home with Miss Smith – to cornflakes, and safety and peace.

Before they settled down for the night, Miss Smith left the back door ajar for a few minutes in case Hilda should feel like stretching her legs. Hilda was longing for a good scratch, but she wasn't very sure about leaving her eggs. She had not quite forgiven Miss Smith for the Victoria sponge! However, Miss Smith promised to look after them *very* carefully, so Hilda popped over the back step and scratched around the little yard. She shook the last of the dust from her feathers before returning to her family.

And before she went to sleep, Miss Smith had a long think about Hilda.

When Mr Biddick came with the milk next morning, Miss Smith asked him in and told him all about Hilda's terrible time in the ruined cottage.

'You will let her hatch the eggs now, won't you, Mr Biddick?' she pleaded.

Mr Biddick rubbed his chin. 'Well, I don't know about that. You see, she's a good little layer, our Hilda, and we can't really afford to let her take time off to rear chicks. They stop laying, you see, that's the trouble.'

Miss Smith made up her mind. 'Mr Biddick, would you consider lending Hilda to me for a while?'

'Lend Hilda to you, Miss Smith? Whatever for?'

'Well, we are just learning about frog spawn and birds' eggs in our Nature class at school. Now if I could *rent* Hilda for a few weeks I could give the children a live lesson –

much better than me trying to draw it on the blackboard.'

'You mean you want to take Hilda to *school*, Miss Smith?'

'Why not? I'm sure Hilda won't mind if it means that she can keep her family. It seems to me to be an excellent plan.'

And that is how Little Dollop School came to have a hen in the classroom – along with three jars of tadpoles and Freddy Hicks' uncle's collection of birds' eggs. Hilda occupied the place of honour in the hole under Miss Smith's desk in front of the class. There she sat in her frying-pan as happy as a queen. Sitting is a boring and lonely business. This was much more fun.

The children thought so too! Hilda became a sort of new girl. They took her out into the playground with them in Break, and shared their elevenses with her (she didn't care for aniseed balls, but popcorn was a different matter). They brought her little presents of worms and rice krispies. They tiptoed about and tried not to shout or bang their desk-lids, so as not to startle her. They had never been so quiet. Miss Smith felt that there was a lot to be said for having a hen in class!

And somehow all the lessons seemed to centre around Hilda. They drew pictures of her for Art. They wrote a composition called 'The hen who came to school' for English. They counted eggs for Arithmetic. They sang 'Please Little Hen' and 'Naughty Little Henny Penny' in the singing lesson. At story time Miss Smith told them about some of Hilda's adventures. These were very popular, particularly the one where Miss Smith and Hilda ended up in a haystack.

In Nature Study they learned about eggs. They learned how the baby chick starts as a tiny speck in the egg, and grows and grows for twenty-one days until it is strong enough to break its way out into the world.

And they all looked at Hilda and wondered when *her* little chicks would begin to break their way out.

One morning when the class was working very quietly making models – of Hilda of course – in plasticine, a little boy in the front row put his hand up.

'I'm sure I can hear tapping, Miss.'

Now this was not unusual. At least a dozen times during the week someone had been sure he or she could hear tapping. But this time when Miss Smith put her ear to the frying-pan, *she* could hear it. She looked up excitedly and spoke to the class.

'Now I want you to come up very quietly and kneel round my desk. No pushing!'

The children came up like little mice and settled around the frying-pan. Hilda was surprised, but pleased to see them. She was completely used to them now.

'Hilda,' Miss Smith said, 'I think your

family is coming. May we have a look?'

Well, of course, Hilda wanted to have a look too, so she raised herself gently off the eggs and stepped back from the frying-pan.

There was an 'Aah!' of disappointment from the children. The eggs looked just the same as usual. Then Miss Smith, asking Hilda for permission, picked up each egg in turn and held it to her ear.

In one of them there was a distinct tapping. She held it for each child to hear, and then put it back carefully with the others.

'Watch!' she whispered.

As they watched, a small crack appeared in the egg, and then a little hole. Now they could see a tiny beak jabbing at the shell from inside. The hole got bigger and bigger – and at last a little damp head squeezed through.

The little chick wriggled and struggled and pushed – until at last it burst the egg right open and fell out.

It didn't move.

'Oh, is it dead?' Jane whispered.

'No, just resting,' said Miss Smith.

Hilda was worried, too. She watched her first chick anxiously. It didn't look right at all – so limp and damp and scrawny. But in a few minutes it was trying out its feet, and as it dried off in the air it began to look as fluffy as a chicken should.

And as cracks appeared in the other eggs and the children began to get very excited, Hilda reached down to welcome her first baby.

She could not quite believe it – until the chick opened its beak and gave its first, strong 'Cheep!'

Then Hilda knew that she had a family
of her very own at last.

This is Suzy.

Suzy is a small stripy cat.

Suzy likes: living in France,
chasing butterflies and being
stroked the wrong way.

Suzy doesn't like: getting lost . . .

Read another Jill Tomlinson
and find out more.

This is Pat.

Pat is a little sea otter.

She loves asking questions.

But what happens when
no one knows the answers?

Clever Pat just has to find
things out for herself!